W9-CDH-577

STUDIO CITY BRANCH LIBRARY
12511 MOORPARK STREET
STUDIO CITY, CALIFORNIA 91604

# old Dry Frye

A DELICIOUSLY FUNNY TALL TALE

# old Dog Cora

STORY AND PICTURES BY PAUL BRETT JOHNSON

SCHOLASTIC INC.
NEW YORK TORONTO LONDON AUCKLAND SYDNEY
MEXICO CITY NEW DELHI HONG KONG

X
398
J675
1999

25 STUDIO CITY

SEP 0 2001

For many years, my mother was an elementary school librarian. Richard Chase's
GRANDFATHER TALES, a collection of Appalachian folk stories, was one of her
favorite books to read from and one of our favorites to listen to. In the gleeful
way that children appreciate dark humor, we especially anticipated
"Old Dry Frye." My telling of this popular romp follows the same
bodacious spirit of the Chase version, if not the letter.

PAUL BRETT JOHNSON
Lexington, Kentucky
December 1998

No part of this publication may be reproduced in whole or in part,
or stored in a retrieval system, or transmitted in any form or by any means,
electronic, mechanical, photocopying, recording, or otherwise,
without written permission of the publisher. For information
regarding permission, write to Scholastic Inc. Attention:
Permissions Department, 555 Broadway, New York, NY 10012.

ISBN 0-439-16392-7

Copyright © 1999 by Paul Brett Johnson.
All rights reserved.
Published by Scholastic Inc.
SCHOLASTIC and associated logos are trademarks and/or registered
trademarks of Scholastic Inc.

12 11 10 9 8 7 6 5 4 3 2 1          1 2 3 4 5 6/0

Printed in the U.S.A.   14

First Scholastic Trade paperback printing, May 2001.

The text type was set in Kosmic Bold.
The display type was set in
Roundhouse and Squarehouse.
The illustrations were painted in acrylics.
Book design by Marijka Kostiw.

**A WHILE BACK** there was this preacher man who was plumb crazy about fried chicken. Now, all preachers like chicken, but Old Dry Frye was the chicken-eatingest sermonizer that ever laid fire to a pulpit.
So if you was having fried chicken for Sunday dinner, you might as well set out an extra plate, 'cause here would come Old Dry Frye with his nose a-twitchin' and his false teeth a-snappin'. You could just count on it.

One time over on Troublesome Creek or thereabouts, Old Dry Frye was making his Sunday rounds. He stopped off at this farmhouse, and his timing couldn't have been better. The folks there had just scooted up their chairs to the dinner table.

EVERYBODY KNEW OLD DRY FRYE, so the wife said, "Howdy, preacher. Would you care for a bite?"

"Why, thank you. Don't mind if I do."

Sad to say, them was Old Dry Frye's last words. He started
gobbling fried chicken so fast he choked on a bone
and died right there on the spot.
Dead as a doornail.
Dead as a
bucket lid.

"Law mercy!" said the husband. "Ain't nobody going to believe Old Dry Frye couldn't put away a plate of chicken. They'll think we killed him. They'll hang us for murder. We got to get shed of him."

So the farmer and his wife took Old Dry Frye up the road to a poor widder woman's hen house. And that's where they left him.

Right away the chickens
commenced squawking and the
rooster crowed its fool head off.
The widder woman come running out
the kitchen door, wielding an iron
skillet. She had been missing a few
chickens lately.

"I'll teach you to stay out of my hen house, you thieving varmint!"
And she walloped Old Dry Frye. The preacher teetered a second and
then just plopped over. The widder woman bent down to get a
better look. Then she let out a big scream.

"Heaven help me! Have I done killed the preacher man?"
EVERYBODY KNEW OLD DRY FRYE.

That widder woman figured she better get shed
of Old Dry Frye in a hurry. Otherwise, she'd be strung
up for murder. She lugged him out of the hen house
and heaped him in a wheelbarrow and lit out down
the hill.

Old Dry Frye weighed a right smart, so the wheelbarrow got to rolling faster and faster. The widder
woman couldn't hardly hold on. All at once the
wheel hit a big rock, and it bounced Old Dry
Frye out of the wheelbarrow and flung him
up in a tree.

"Well, there's a piece of luck," said the
widder woman, and she went back home.

That evening after dark, there was two brothers
coming home late. They stopped to rest underneath
the tree. One of them happened to look up, and he
saw two big round eyes shining in the moonlight.
"Lookey there," he said. "Hit's a big fat possum!
I wouldn't mind having me some possum stew for supper."
So the brother found himself a smooth rock. He
rared back, sighted, and let go.

Well, here come Old Dry Frye tumbling down out of that
tree, and he smacked the ground in front of them.
"Mighty big possum," said the other brother, and
he went over to take a look. "Why, this ain't
no possum a-tall. Hit's Old Dry Frye.
You done killed the preacher man!"
EVERYBODY KNEW OLD DRY FRYE.
"Sakes alive! What're we gonna do?" said the first brother.
"Whatta you mean WE?" said the other brother. "You was the
one that killed him. They'll prob'ly send you to the pen."
"Oh, you gotta help me, brother." So the two of them carried Old
Dry Frye home with them. They tied him up in a feed sack and
throwed him in the creek. They figured that would be the
end of Old Dry Frye, and nobody would be the wiser.

But the preacher man didn't sink to the bottom like he was
supposed to. Old Dry Frye washed downstream a ways till he
got snagged beside the creek bank.
The next day here come this feller with a sack full of
hog meat. The sack was heavy and the sun was beaming down.
The feller was puffing like a blacksmith and the sweat was rolling,
so he decided to take a dip in the creek to cool off. He laid his sack
alongside the creek and took off his clothes and jumped in.

The feller was having such a fine time,
he didn't notice that his sack of hog meat had
slid off the bank into the creek and floated away.
When he felt good and cool, he got out, put his clothes
back on, and looked around for his sack.
"Now, where did I put that dadburn hog meat?" he wondered.
Directly the feller saw a big sack snagged by the bank. "Reckon
how it got down there?" He hefted the sack and went on his way.
It seemed a bit heavier than it used to. When he got home, he
hung up the sack in the smokehouse.

The next morning, the feller's wife went out to the
smokehouse to slice some bacon for breakfast. She
opened the sack, and out tumbled Old Dry Frye! She
hollered and squalled till her husband come running out
to see what the commotion was.

"This ain't no sack of hog meat! Hit's Old Dry Frye!" she screamed.
EVERYBODY KNEW OLD DRY FRYE.

Well, there wasn't but one thing to do: They had to get shed
of Old Dry Frye before somebody accused them of murder.
They had a mean-spirited horse that wasn't much 'count, so
they put Old Dry Frye a-top him. They took a broom and slapped
that horse on the rear end. The horse tore out down the
road like a train running late. Old Dry Frye bounced
and bucked from side to side with
his chin a-bobbin' and his
elbows a-flappin'.

The man and his wife started yelling, "Thief, thief! Stop that horse thief! He stole our best horse!" Folks come running out of their houses and tried to catch up with that wild horse, but it wasn't any use. In less time than it takes to tell it, Old Dry Frye was spotted down around Monkey's Eyebrow.

They say Old Dry Frye is still tearing around the countryside. On nights when the moon is full and there's a plate of chicken on the table, you can guess what folks are saying:

"Dad-fetch me! I believe that's Old Dry Frye."